STAR OF WONDER

Written by MARY LEE WILE · *Illustrated by* SAGE STOSSEL

Forward Movement
Cincinnati, Ohio

Illustrations by Sage Stossel

Book design: Albonetti Design

ISBN 978-0-88028-345-8

Library of Congress Control Number: 2012940473

Printed in USA

Forward Movement
412 Sycamore Street
Cincinnati, Ohio 45202-4195
www.forwardmovement.org

STAR
OF
WONDER

Written by MARY LEE WILE • *Illustrated by* SAGE STOSSEL

For our entire extended family,
the Hanford, Wile, Brown, Callaghan, Stossel clan,
especially the youngest generation.

MARY LEE WILE & SAGE STOSSEL

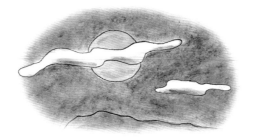

The young shepherd Jesse shivered as night fell and clouds seemed to eat up the moon. He had been proud when his father said,

"You're a big boy now and can tend the sheep on your own."

But it was different at night. He knew there were other shepherds nestled with their flocks behind nearby hills, but he felt alone.

It was very cold and dark.

Then something flashed above his head in the sky, startling him.

"What was that?" he wondered.

He lifted his face and saw, in the darkness, a light!

It was a star, bigger and brighter than any he'd ever seen,
shining right through the clouds.

All at once Jesse felt his heart warmed by the light
of the star, and the sky began to sing.

Amazed, he settled against a rock and enjoyed
the beauty of the star, and the woolly sheep, and
the glory of the deep winter's night.

He wasn't afraid any more.

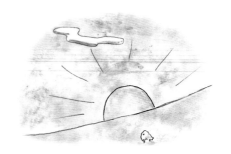

Early the next morning, Jesse's brother came racing
up the hill, swooped up one of the lambs in his arms,
and danced around the fire.

"You'll never guess what happened last night!" he said.

"You mean the star?" Jesse asked. "I saw it, too!"

"But you didn't see the baby!"

"What baby?" Jesse asked.

"God's baby," his brother Daniel answered. "A tiny baby asleep in the old stable by the inn. And there were angels there who said he was God's own Son."

"You saw angels?" Jesse asked.

"No," Daniel answered. "But I heard them."

Then Jesse knew why the night sky had been singing.

For eleven days and eleven nights,
Jesse watched the bright star in the winter
sky and waited for angels to sing again.

But they never did.

On the twelfth night as he kept watch over the flock, snow drifted down and dusted the field and the sleeping sheep. The surrounding hills were humped like camels, looking shaggy and brown by the light of the star that shone through falling snow.

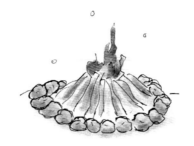

Jesse sat by the warming fire and pressed his palm
into the soft snow, making a shape like a star.

Suddenly, some of the hills began to move. Looking
closer, Jesse saw that these hills really were camels.
They plodded through the snow slowly, as though old
and tired as the hills themselves. As they drew closer
and closer to the fire, Jesse saw three strange men
trudging along beside them.

One of the men was dressed in purple and as dark as the night except for his eyes, which shone bright with excitement.

Another man was very tall. He was wearing a rich red robe and had a long braid all the way down his back.

The third wore a royal blue turban wrapped around his head.

Hugging his woolen cloak around him, Jesse rose to greet the strangers.

The man with the turban said, "Young shepherd, can you help us?
We've followed the star through the desert, over many mountains,
and across the sea."

He pointed to the great star in the sky.

The man with the shining eyes said,

"This star is leading us to the Holy Child.
He will grow up to be the Savior of the world.
He is God's own Son."

The tall man said, "We've come bringing gifts for him."

Jesse noticed all the packages piled on the sturdy camels.

"The star shines over his birthplace," said the dark man with bright eyes. "Can you take us there?"

Jesse thought of his brother's story of a baby born in a stable.

"I think so," he said. "We can go there at first light when my brother comes to take my place."

So the travelers tethered the camels to a tree
and removed their burdens. They gave
the camels hay to eat and water to drink and
covered them with warm woolen blankets.
Then they joined Jesse at the fire.

As sparks from the fire rose to meet the falling
snow, the boy broke bread with the weary men,
and the bright star kept on shining.

One by one the men wrapped themselves in
their robes of purple and red and royal blue,
and laid themselves down to sleep.

Jesse kept watch over the men and the sheep
as night moved on toward dawn.

When the first grey light of morning softened
the sky, Jesse's brother was surprised to find
camels grazing with the sheep and strangers
eating breakfast by the fire.

When Daniel heard their story, he said to Jesse,
"Now you'll get to see the baby, too!"

After helping pack up the camels,
Jesse led the travelers on the road to Bethlehem.

They came at last to a small stable, tucked between a crooked olive tree and an old inn.

As they approached the stable, Jesse heard the rustle of wings and knew angels must be nearby. He looked up at the star, still shining in the morning light.

Jesse followed the three men through the doorway,
into the warmth of the stable. He saw sheep and cows
moving like shadows in the dim light.

The travelers knelt beside a manger where a baby
slept amid the straw. A man and a woman stood beside
them, gazing at the sleeping Child. Golden light
surrounded the Child, and Jesse's heart felt warm.

He felt just as he had the first night he saw the star.

Outside, the star flickered…

...and faded away.

Inside, the Child awoke, uncurled his tiny fist, and reached his hand toward Jesse. The warmth in Jesse's heart deepened as he took the tiny hand into his own.

Holding that hand was like holding the star itself!

In all the years that followed, Jesse never forgot the touch of the Holy Child's hand. Even when he grew up and had flocks and children of his own, every time Jesse looked at the night sky, he thought of the bright star.

And in his warm and happy heart,
he knew God still held him by the hand.

Star of Wonder *shares the mystery and excitement of the season of Epiphany.*

For more background on the season and for ways to celebrate Epiphany visit:

WWW.STAROFWONDEREPIPHANY.COM